Kealy Connor Lonning

Your Mama
LOVES YOU

Illustrator Lora Look

D1558601

Your mama loves you bright—
like golden rays of sun.
I'll share your hopes and dreams—
and fill your life with fun.

Sea Lions—
Galapagos Islands

Red Panda

Your mama loves you great.
I'll teach you everything.
The world sure needs you here.
What blessings you will bring.

Your mama loves you tall.
It's hard to measure right.
For you're my gift, my charm,
my treasure, my delight.

Kordofan Giraffe

Chimpanzee

Your mama loves you wild—
the way you climb and play.
I'll squeeze you with my hugs,
as we enjoy each day.

Your mama loves you deep.
I'm thrilled to be your guide.
And we are full of joy,
when we are side by side.

Blue Whale

Your mama loves you soft.
Each kiss and hug and touch,
makes cuddling you the best.
I love you very much.

Giant Panda

Your mama loves you high—
I'll give you every chance,
for many special times,
and you will learn to dance.

Whooping Crane

Red Wolf

Your mama loves you wide—
just like the endless sky.
I'll always care for you,
and keep you warm and dry.

Your mama loves you grand.
You make me super proud.
We'll love through smiles and tears,
and when you're shy or loud.

Orangutan

Javan Rhinoceros

Your mama loves you brave –
we'll practice being strong,
and as you're getting big,
I'll teach you right from wrong.

Your mama loves you fierce—
if trouble is around,
you know I'm here for you,
to keep you safe and sound.

Sumatran Tiger

Your mama loves you sweet.
We'll work on being kind.
I'll show you how to love,
and many friends you'll find.

Sea Otter

Your mama loves you far—
like shining stars at night.
I'll tuck you into bed,
and make sure you're alright.

Amur Leopard

Sumatran Elephant

Your mama loves you wise.
I hope you'll always know--
my love will follow you,
through all the years you grow.

I love you for all time,
and if we're far apart,
your mama's love won't stop.
You're always in my heart.

A Note from the Author

I was so excited to create this book with my amazing illustrator! My wonderful parents taught me to care for people, animals, and the Earth. I believe that wildlife and the environment need our help.

We live on a spectacular planet, with fascinating plants and animals. Each one is a vital part of its ecosystem. The heartbreaking loss of a species can affect others, as well as humans.

Sadly, many creatures across the globe, face a high risk of extinction in the near future. They are considered to be Vulnerable, Endangered, or Critically Endangered. A species can become threatened for many reasons, such as habitat loss, poaching, and pollution.

The Endangered Species Act (ESA) was established to protect and help species and ecosystems recover. There are many international organizations, governments, communities, and individuals, working together, toward conservation of them.

I hope this gorgeous book will increase awareness of endangered animals. May these beautiful mamas and babies, inspire you to learn more about them. We all can find ways to help. One way is to share our knowledge with others, and the importance of preserving these species, for future generations.

Dedication

For my beautiful, amazing, MAMA, Micki Stirn Connor, who showed me how to be an awesome MOM. I am so fortunate! My mom and dad/Jim, gave me and my two sisters a glorious childhood. Our life was filled with unconditional love, compassion, literacy, learning, and fun. Mom was, and still is, the perfect role model--positive, kind, humble, smart, diligent, brave, and strong!

Mom is a caretaker--selfless, compassionate, and generous, and has always helped others. As a registered nurse, she helped even more. Mom is a humanitarian, with integrity to do what is right. Even as a girl, she risked her own privileges, to defend the oppressed, and promote social justice.

I love how Mom always finds joy and beauty in ordinary days, and in simple things! She taught me to be grateful, graceful, and confident, and she still gives me wise advice. I am thankful for her many sacrifices, and devotion to our entire family--she is the best NANA. My mom has saved my self-esteem many times, and believed in me, giving me hope and courage, to follow my dreams! ♥

For my six beautiful, delightful CHILDREN, who made me a MAMA! They inspire me to write books, as they showed me how simple wonders of childhood are magical. Being their MOM has taught me so much, and I learned how boundless love can be. My kids are my legacy, and their dad/Greg, and I are blessed to be their parents. They are all multi-talented, and we are super proud of them! We have raised "our champions" to be kind, strong, brave, and grateful. We encourage them to find their passions, chase their dreams, and change the world! 😍

**Your Mama Loves You--
Connor, Moran, Gable, Gara, Summer, & Shanae**
🖤 "You're always in my heart." 🖤

Like this book?
Please consider leaving
a review online.

Available on
Amazon.com

Facebook/Instagram:
AuthorKealyConnorLonning
KealyConnor0716@gmail.com

Books by Kealy Connor Lonning

Kealy Connor Lonning
Our Wonderful You
Illustrator Lora Look

Kealy Connor Lonning
Our Mighty You
Illustrator Lora Look

Follow Your Dreams

The Wonders of Childhood

Kealy Connor Lonning
OUR AMAZING BLANKETS
Illustrator Lora Look

Kealy Connor Lonning
THE WONDERS OF SUMMER
Illustrator Lora Look

Kealy Connor Lonning
I Love You More Than All
Illustrator Lora Look

Kealy Connor Lonning
Your Mama LOVES YOU
Illustrator Lora Look

Kealy Connor Lonning
HOPE
Illustrator Lora Look

Be Kind and Brave

Made in United States
North Haven, CT
03 December 2022

27760966R00022